MILLIE COOPER, 3B

by Charlotte Herman

illustrated by Helen Cogancherry

E. P. DUTTON   NEW YORK

Library of Congress Cataloging in Publication Data

Herman, Charlotte.
  Millie Cooper, 3B.
  Summary: As she tries to cope with school and other
problems, third-grader Millie discovers some special
things about herself.
  1. Children's stories, American. [1. Self-perception
—Fiction. 2. Schools—Fiction] I. Title. II. Title:
Millie Cooper, Three B.
PZ7.H4313Mi 1985 [Fic] 84-25951
ISBN 0-525-44157-3

Published in the United States by E. P. Dutton,
2 Park Avenue, New York, N.Y. 10016,
a subsidiary of NAL Penguin Inc.

Published simultaneously in Canada by
Fitzhenry & Whiteside Limited, Toronto

Editor: Julie Amper   Designer: Isabel Warren-Lynch

Printed in the U.S.A.   W
10 9 8 7 6 5 4

remembering
my mother and father,
Leah and Harry Baran,
who left me so many
special memories

Contents

1

The Spelling Test

Millie Cooper sat at her desk. She hurried to complete the heading on the long, narrow spelling-test paper before Miss Brennan shouted out her orders. She wrote:

*Millicent Cooper
Grade 3B   Room 210
Lawson School
November 8, 1946
Spelling Test*

Millie thought it was a stupid heading. So many wasted words. Why did she have to write *Lawson School*? Didn't Miss Brennan know what school she was teaching in? And why did Millie have to write *Spelling Test*? Anyone could see it was a spelling test just by looking at it. She numbered her paper from one to twenty-five as Miss Brennan walked up to the front of the room.

"Everybody fill your fountain pens. There will be no stopping for anyone who dries up in the middle of the test."

Millie already had her pen filled with royal blue ink, so she just sat back and watched the other kids reaching into their desks for their ink bottles or filling their pens from their inkwells. Only Marlene Kaufman didn't need any ink. She had one of those new ballpoint pens that just came out. A Reynolds Rocket. What a wonderful invention. Imagine! A pen that writes easily like a pencil, only ink comes out of it instead of lead. Millie eyed the Rocket with envy. Long, sleek, and shiny silver. How she wished she had one. Then there would be no more bottles of ink, no more overflowing inkwells to spill out all over your books and papers, no more royal blue hands.

"Get ready now for your twenty-five farm words," said Miss Brennan. She was standing in front of the class, holding the list of spelling words. "And remember, use ink only. No pencils. There is to be no erasing, no crossing out, no ink blots, or you get a zero on the whole test. And neatness counts."

Millie swallowed hard and wiped her sweaty

palms on her skirt. These tests always made her nervous. It wasn't that she couldn't spell. She was a good speller, and she always knew the words. Last year when she was in the second grade, she surprised her teacher by spelling *formaldehyde* correctly in a composition. Millie knew all about that awful-smelling formaldehyde. She had a cousin who was studying to be a doctor, and he used formaldehyde to keep dead cats from going bad.

But even if you were a good speller, it was so easy to make a mistake. So easy to add a wrong letter or to leave a letter out. And once you realized your mistake, it was too late. Miss Brennan didn't allow corrections. Even without spelling mistakes, just a slip of the pen and . . .

"I don't want to see anybody writing until I've said the word, the sentence, and the word again," said Miss Brennan. "Now, begin. Number one: *tractor.* The farmer plowed the field with a tractor. *Tractor.*"

In one motion, as if the word came out of heaven itself, everyone leaned over to write *tractor.* Millie was careful to write each letter slowly and clearly. She blew on the word so it would dry before it had a chance to get smeared.

"Number two," said Miss Brennan, "is *oatmeal.* Everyone should eat oatmeal for breakfast. *Oatmeal.*"

The whole class groaned at the thought of eating oatmeal for breakfast, but everyone wrote the word. Everyone, that is, except for O.C. Goodwin. O.C. Goodwin was not good. He was a class troublemaker.

"*Oatmeal* isn't a farm word," O.C. called out.

"People on farms eat oatmeal, too, dummy," said Howard Hall, who was another class troublemaker.

Miss Brennan didn't say anything, but she shut them both up with a cold stare.

Miss Brennan called off the words one by one, and Millie wrote each word neatly and correctly. Word number fifteen was *cabbage,* and O.C. asked if that word was spelled with one *b* or two. Miss Brennan almost told him. After Miss Brennan announced the twentieth word, *barley,* Howard Hall asked her if she would repeat word number three.

"No repeats," said Miss Brennan. "You must learn to listen."

Millie was relieved when Miss Brennan called out the last word. Word number twenty-five. "*Soil.* Farmers need good soil for their crops to grow. *Soil.*"

Millie was delighted. *Soil* was an easy word. She knew how to spell it. Slowly and carefully she started to write. But somewhere between the *s* and the *o,* a drop of ink just dripped out of her pen and onto her paper. Frantically Millie searched

4

her desk for a blotter so she could soak up the ink. She pressed the blotter on the ink drop, afraid to see what was underneath. When she looked, she felt sick. Not only did *soil* turn into an ink blot, but the blot spread to word number twenty-four, *stable.*

"Will the last person in each row collect the papers?" Miss Brennan called out.

Millie didn't know what to do. She felt like hiding in the cloakroom behind the coats. She couldn't hand in a paper with ink blots and get a zero on the test. It wasn't fair—not when she knew all the words.

She picked up her test and slowly walked to the front of the room where Miss Brennan was standing, looking bigger and meaner than ever, with her thick brown hair that everyone said was a wig.

"Miss Brennan," said Millie in a very small voice. "My pen . . ." She pointed to the blots.

"I suppose you'll have to be more careful next time," said Miss Brennan.

"But I *was* careful, and I know how to spell the words. It's just that . . ." Millie felt her lips begin to quiver.

Stop it, she told herself. Don't cry. Not in front of *Miss Brennan.* But she couldn't stop her eyes from filling up. And when Miss Brennan took Millie's test away, the tears started to spill out.

Millie turned away and went back to her seat,

angry and disappointed in herself. She no longer cared about the spelling test. She no longer cared about the zero. But why did she have to cry?

When she was in the second grade, she had cried a lot. And when she began third grade, she made herself a promise. No more crying in front of teachers. She would never ever give them the satisfaction of seeing her cry. Not Millie Cooper. But here she was, doing it again.

2

Am I Special?

Millie's favorite place to read, write, or think was on the window seat in the kitchen. From there she could look out over the courtyard at the backs of the other apartment buildings. And at the same time she could be with her mother in the kitchen— where it was warm and cozy and always smelled of cinnamon and vanilla because her mother did so much cooking and baking.

On the Monday after that awful spelling test, Millie took her place on the window seat as soon as she came home from school and had something to eat. She had to do some serious thinking. Miss Brennan had asked everyone to write a composition on "Why I Am Special." The composition was due after Thanksgiving vacation, just three weeks away.

Millie couldn't think of anything that was special about her—except that she was born in June. Millie thought that the word *June* had a nice sound to it. Yet, somehow she didn't feel that she should get any credit for something she had nothing to do with.

"Mama," Millie asked, "am I special?"

"Of course you are," said Mrs. Cooper as she grated potatoes into chopped meat.

"How?" asked Millie.

"You're a very good, kind, and sweet young lady," said Mrs. Cooper.

That was just the kind of thing she'd expect her mother to say. Millie could picture herself writing in her composition, *I am special because I'm a very good, kind, and sweet young lady, and I was born in June.*

"Mama, I can't write that. I need something better."

"There's nothing better than being good, kind, and sweet," said her mother, who was now crying because of the onions she was grating into the chopped meat.

Millie was glad that her mother thought she was good, kind, and sweet, but she knew she'd have to think of something else to write.

She picked up her pencil and opened her loose-leaf notebook to a fresh page. She titled it:

*Why I Am Special
by Millie Cooper*

She'd have to change *Millie* to *Millicent* on her final copy. Miss Brennan insisted on full names. She didn't allow nicknames or shortened forms—except for O.C., whose initials didn't stand for anything. But for now, Millie could write her name any way she liked.

After she finished writing her name, Millie couldn't think of anything else to write. She stared at the white page in front of her.

In the margins she drew little squares and boxes and shaded them in. Around the boxes she drew stars—both five-pointed and six-pointed ones. Doodling sometimes gave her inspiration, but not today. What she needed, she was certain, was the Reynolds Rocket. With a pen like that, she could write the best composition in class, the best composition in the whole Victor Lawson Elementary School.

The aroma of hamburgers frying filled the kitchen. Millie looked up to see her mother shaping a blob of the meat mixture into a ball, then flattening it out into a patty. Millie jumped off the window seat and went over to the stove to help with the cooking. She liked to make herself very tiny patties. Baby hamburgers, she called them. She'd fry them and eat them as soon as they were done.

"Mama, you know what I need?" Millie asked

as she rolled a baby hamburger between her hands.

"What is it this time?" asked Mrs. Cooper.

"A new pen."

"What's wrong with the one you have?"

"It leaks. Look what it did to my spelling test last Friday."

Millie had told her mother all about her ink blots and her zero. The only part she left out was the crying.

"What I need is one of those new ballpoint pens," said Millie. "A Reynolds Rocket."

"Wait until they're perfected," said Mrs. Cooper. "I'm sure they don't work very well yet."

"Sure they work. Everyone has one."

"Who's everyone?"

"Marlene Kaufman."

"As I said, wait until they're perfected. I hate to throw money down the drain."

Millie could see that she wasn't going to get anywhere with her mother. She'd ask her father during supper. He wasn't so practical.

Millie put her baby hamburgers on a plate and went into the dining room so she could eat them while she listened to the radio. She sat down on the floor just as Wheaties, Breakfast of Champions, was presenting "Jack Armstrong, the All-American Boy." She listened as the announcer told how everybody could be just like Jack Armstrong if they followed his simple training program—which included plenty of fresh air and exercise, lots of soap and water, and a big bowl of Wheaties with milk or cream. That training program might have helped Jack Armstrong become special, Millie thought, but she doubted that it would help her.

Somewhere between "Jack Armstrong" and "The Lone Ranger," Millie's father came home from work. She didn't notice him until he walked into the dining room with his hat and coat still on and the newspaper tucked under his arm. Millie and her mother went over to greet him, and the three of them walked into the kitchen.

"I was starting to get worried about you," said Mrs. Cooper. Millie's mother always worried about her father if he didn't get home by six o'clock.

"I got tied up in traffic," said Mr. Cooper, handing Millie the newspaper and taking off his hat and coat. "Boy, it's getting nasty out there. I wouldn't be surprised if we get some snow tonight."

"Oh, Daddy, do you really think so?" Millie couldn't wait to unroll the paper and check the weather forecast on the front page of the *Chicago Daily News*. Every evening since the beginning of November, she looked hopefully for the words *snow flurries.* But so far there had been no snow in the forecast. There was none this evening either.

Millie decided it would be best to ask her father about the Rocket after he finished supper. On days that he got tied up in traffic, it took him longer to get into a good mood. Millie even ate her tomato soup without complaining. Millie hated tomato soup, but for some crazy reason that she could never figure out, tomato soup was one of the few foods Mrs. Cooper forced upon her.

Millie dunked six saltine squares into her soup. The crackers soaked up the soup and made it disappear from the bowl like magic. Now all Millie had to do was eat the crackers. She could hardly taste the soup.

After some boring conversation about trouble with the help in her father's furniture factory and getting the orders out on time, Mrs. Cooper got up to clear the table and carry the dishes over to the sink. Mr. Cooper sat back in his chair and let out a contented sigh. This was clearly the time to ask.

"Daddy," Millie said, "can I get a ballpoint pen?"

"Why?" asked Mr. Cooper.

"You can't imagine the trouble I've been having with my fountain pen lately. And I've got a special composition coming up pretty soon, and I could write it better if I had a ballpoint."

"I've heard that they don't work all that well.

I've heard that they leak, they skip, and they goop."

"But everyone's got one."

"Who's everyone?"

"Marlene Kaufman," said Mrs. Cooper as she came back for more dishes. "Do you know what those pens must cost? Five dollars at least. If you ask me, it's just an extravagant gimmick."

"But it'll be a good investment," Millie argued. "It's guaranteed for fifteen years or thirty-two miles, whichever comes first. Think of that. I can get stranded on an island for fifteen years and never have to worry about filling my pen. Look at all the money we'll save on ink. And anyway, I've got two dollars of my own, and the rest of the money could be my birthday present we never got around to buying."

"We'll see," said Mr. Cooper, and he picked up the *Daily News* and went into the dining room.

"It writes underwater," Millie called after him. But her father didn't seem to hear.

We'll see. That could mean anything. Yes. No. Maybe. It was not the answer Millie had hoped for.

Millie waited until her mother and father finished listening to Gabriel Heatter on the eight o'clock news before she said good-night. Millie liked the beginning of the program—when Gabriel

14

Heatter said, "Ah, there's good news tonight." After that, she couldn't understand what he was talking about.

"Daddy," Millie asked when the news was over. "Am I special?"

"Of course you are," said her father, putting his arms around her.

"How?"

"You just are, that's all. You're my little girl, and that makes you special."

Very nice. But again, nothing she could write in her composition.

Just before she was ready to climb into bed, Millie looked out the window into the night. The wind was blowing a lone piece of paper across the street, and Millie followed it with her eyes until it disappeared. She looked up at the light coming from a street lamp on the corner and watched for snowflakes, wishing hard that they'd come. For a moment she thought she saw a snowflake fall, but it was just a piece of dust. Up in the sky a far-off star winked at her, and Millie closed her eyes to make a wish. It was an exceptionally bright star. She would make three wishes.

"Star light, star bright," whispered Millie, "first star I see tonight . . ." And on that one star, Millie wished for a Reynolds Rocket and snow and a way to figure out how she was special. She opened her eyes to see the star coming closer and closer until it traveled across the sky away from her.

"Oh, nuts," said Millie, pulling down the window shade. "I just wished on an airplane."

3

Too Early for Lunch

It was just after nine o'clock the next morning, and Millie was starving. She reached into her desk and felt around for something to eat. An old pistachio nut maybe. Or a leftover Milk Dud. But all she came up with was a lemon Life Saver covered with red glitter. She stuck it back in her desk. Hungry as she was, she was not desperate enough to eat a glitter-coated Life Saver.

How she wished she had eaten the Cream of Wheat her mother had prepared for her. But Millie woke up later than she usually did, and there wasn't time to eat a single spoonful.

Millie was so hungry she could hardly concentrate on the multiplication tables she was supposed to be working on. She had to write the sixes' table four times.

In the seat in front of Millie, her best friend, Sandy Feinman, was busy folding her arithmetic paper into four columns. She seemed to be trying very hard to get the folds perfectly even. Anything to keep from working on the problems.

Millie and Sandy had been best friends since first grade. They were both the tallest and thinnest girls in the class, and were weeds in last year's school play. All the short, cute girls were flowers. Millie and Sandy were also candidates for braces. That's what the dentist told their mothers. To Millie, it sounded like a great honor—to be a candidate for braces. Actually it just meant that they both had overbites and would probably need braces on their teeth in two or three years.

Millie folded a sheet of arithmetic paper into four columns, and on it she wrote a note to Sandy: *Do you have any food?* She passed the note while Miss Brennan was busy yelling at somebody for going to the wastebasket without permission.

Sandy read the note and sent it back saying: *No, but I'll take a walk and ask around for some.*

Millie watched as Sandy broke the point of her pencil on her desk. Then she raised her hand and waited for Miss Brennan to notice her.

Millie knew what Sandy planned to do. Sandy often pretended that her pencil needed sharpening, when all she wanted was an excuse to get up and walk around the room. The sharpener was at the back of the room by the window. Millie and Sandy sat toward the front of the room by the door. So it was a nice long walk. Along the way

Sandy could ask if anyone had something to eat.

"Yes, Miss Feinman?" Miss Brennan said. Millie hated it when teachers called kids by their last names.

"Miss Brennan," said Sandy, "may I please sharpen my pencil?" Sandy held the pencil in the air so Miss Brennan would see how badly it needed sharpening.

"No you may not, Miss Feinman. I'm well aware of your little tricks."

As soon as Miss Brennan's back was turned, Sandy stuck out her tongue. Millie giggled. Then Sandy giggled. Then they both started laughing harder. Millie laughed into her desk so Miss Brennan couldn't see her. She pretended to be looking for something. She had such a good time laughing, she almost forgot about being hungry.

When she gained control of herself, Millie returned to her multiplication tables. She folded a new piece of arithmetic paper into four columns. Across the top of the paper, she wrote another stupid heading.

Millicent Cooper   November 12, 1946
Grade 3B   Room 210   Lawson School
Arithmetic

Down the first column she made a row of sixes, then a row of X's, a row of numbers from zero to twelve, then a row of equal signs. She began to do the same thing in the other columns. She left out the answers because that was the hard part. She'd have to go back and work on them later.

Millie looked at Sandy's paper and saw that she was making a row of equal signs. Sandy didn't have any answers either, only problems. No wonder they were best friends.

When the bell finally rang, Millie lined up right away so she could be the first one out of the building. Usually she waited for Sandy, and they walked home together for lunch. But today she was too hungry to wait. As soon as she was out the door, Millie ran towards home. As she was running, she thought about the Cream of Wheat and wondered if it was still waiting for her.

When Millie was about a block from home, she looked around and noticed that the streets were empty. Where were all the kids? They were probably way behind her. She never realized what a fast runner she was. She was beating the whole school home for lunch. Maybe being a fast runner made her special. Maybe that was something she could write in her composition. The thought so delighted Millie, she ran even faster.

Millie entered her building through the front

door because it was closer than the back door. She paused briefly in the hallway to look through the slots in her mailbox, which was lined up with five others along the wall. It was dark inside. No white envelopes showed through. And since she hadn't sent away for anything recently, there were no small packages either.

Millie rang the bell and ran up the flight of stairs.

"Hi," she said when her mother opened the door.

"Hi," said Mrs. Cooper. "What are you doing home?"

Millie was surprised by her mother's question. She was home for lunch, of course.

"I'm home for lunch, of course," said Millie.

"At ten fifteen?"

"Ten fifteen? You mean it's not lunchtime?"

Her mother shook her head.

"You mean . . . it's recess time?"

Her mother nodded.

"Oh, no," said Millie, and she turned and ran down the stairs and out the door. How dumb, thought Millie. How stupid. She was not a fast runner at all. She was not special, just stupid.

Millie ran to school even faster than she had run home. Her chest was hurting, and she had a hard time breathing. But she kept on running.

Maybe she could still get back in time and catch up with the kids as they were filing into the school. Maybe they didn't even notice she was gone. Sandy would have noticed, though. Millie would tell her that she went to get something to eat. She just wouldn't say how far she went.

The schoolyard was packed with kids, but they all looked older. It was probably the second recess, the big kids' recess. Millie ran up to a girl who was standing near the fence.

"Excuse me," said Millie, "but is this . . . is this the big kids' recess?"

"Yeah," said the girl.

It was too late. Now Millie would have to tell Miss Brennan what happened, and the whole class would know she went home for recess. Unless, of course, she could tell Miss Brennan in a whisper.

Millie raced into the building and up the stairs. She stood outside Room 210 for a few seconds while she caught her breath, then opened the door. Miss Brennan was seated at her desk. She looked up when Millie walked in.

"You're late, Miss Cooper."

"I'm sorry," said Millie, "but—"

"You may sit down," said Miss Brennan.

Millie walked up to her teacher to whisper her excuse. "Miss Brennan, I thought—"

"Sit," said Miss Brennan, pointing to Millie's desk.

So Millie sat. There was nothing else she could do. She bent down and pretended to be tying her laces so nobody would see the tears coming. She was doing it again—crying. Like a baby.

What was wrong with her anyway? And what was wrong with Miss Brennan? She wouldn't even listen to Millie. She was one of those teachers who never listened. She herself had told Howard Hall, "You must learn to listen," but she never did. You're late, Miss Cooper. In her thoughts Millie imitated the way Miss Brennan had said that to her.

"Sometimes I think I hate her," Millie told Sandy when they were walking home during the real lunch hour. Millie had just finished telling Sandy how she ran home for recess. She decided to tell her because Sandy was, after all, her best friend. What good was a best friend if you couldn't tell her the truth once in a while? And Sandy really was a best friend. She didn't even laugh at Millie.

"Sometimes I think I hate her," Millie repeated, "and then I feel sorry for her."

"How can you hate someone and feel sorry for her at the same time?" Sandy asked.

"I guess I feel sorry for her because there's someone like me who hates her so much."

They crossed Central Park Avenue and headed

down Thirteenth Street. "You know what I do when Miss Brennan gets me mad?" Sandy said. "I just think of her wig and that boy with the window pole."

Ever since first grade, Millie had been hearing the story of a boy who once lifted off Miss Brennan's wig with a window pole and left her standing in front of the whole class with her bald head. Nobody seemed to know who the boy was or when this whole thing was supposed to have happened, but the story was told and retold year after year.

"You should try it sometime," Sandy suggested. "You'll be so busy laughing at her in your mind, you won't even care what she says to you."

Ordinarily Millie would never think of laughing at somebody just because she was bald or wore a wig. It wasn't all that funny. But when it came to Miss Brennan, it was different. Millie didn't think it would be such a bad thing to laugh at Miss Brennan in her mind. She deserved it.

"I'll try it the next time she's mean to me," said Millie. "And not only will I imagine her bald, but I'll imagine her naked, too."

Millie and Sandy burst out laughing at the same time. Then they linked arms and walked down Thirteenth Street together.

4

One Way To Be Special

"I was really proud of what Millie did this morning," Mrs. Cooper told Mr. Cooper over tea that evening.

Millie heard this as she was sitting on the dining-room floor cutting out an ad for the Reynolds Rocket from the newspaper. The ad showed a picture of the Rocket and listed the six glorious colors you could choose from. Millie had already decided on Chute Silver, like the one Marlene Kaufman had. But she would have been satisfied with any of the colors, especially Cosmic Gold or Stratosphere Blue.

"You're proud of the way I came home for recess?" Millie asked.

"No, I'm proud of the way you went back to school," said her mother. "I watched from the window as you were running back. I knew you were in a hurry, and I was worried. But I didn't have to be. I saw the way you stopped at each corner and looked both ways before you crossed the street."

"Well, I'm glad to hear that, Millie," said Mr. Cooper. "I'm proud of you, too."

Millie imagined writing in her composition: *I am special because I look both ways before I cross the street, even when I'm in a hurry.* No, that wasn't going to work.

"Are you proud enough to get me a Rocket?" Millie asked.

"Believe me," said Mrs. Cooper, "it's a waste of money."

"We'll have to think about it some more," said Mr. Cooper.

Millie decided that her mother and father could use some help with their thinking. And she wanted them to see that the pen didn't cost five dollars. It was only three dollars and ninety-eight cents, plus tax.

Millie placed the newspaper ad on the kitchen table and kept it there while they remained in the kitchen. Later she followed them into the dining room and placed the ad next to the radio, so they could see it when they changed stations. To help remind them even further, Millie walked around the apartment singing her Rocket song:

Got a Rocket in your pocket?
If you do, don't sock it.
Or you won't have a Rocket
In your pocket
Anymore.

Millie longed for the day when she could sing that song with a real Rocket in her pocket.

"Don't you think Chute Silver is a nicer color for a pen than Jet Black or Radar Green?" Millie asked her father before she went to bed. She felt that it couldn't hurt to drop an extra hint or two once in a while.

"I think it's an even nicer color for a pen than Atomic Red," Mr. Cooper said, and he smiled at her.

Millie smiled back. Not only had he read the ad, but he knew the colors, too.

Millie picked out her clothes for the next day and climbed into bed. The room was cold and so were the sheets. She crawled under the covers and curled herself up into a little ball. Mrs. Cooper came in a few minutes later with an extra blanket.

"I think you'll need this tonight," she said, tucking the blanket around the little ball. "The temperature is supposed to drop."

Millie poked her head out. "Do you think it'll snow tonight?"

"It might. When it comes to Chicago's weather, you never can tell."

"I hope we at least get some snow for Thanksgiving," Millie said. She loved cold, cloudy Thanksgiving days—with just a light snow falling.

The extra blanket helped, and with her mother sitting beside her, Millie felt warm and safe. "Mama," Millie asked, "what does it mean if a person cries a lot?"

"It might mean that the person is unhappy about something," her mother said.

"What if this person is really happy? But she cries when a teacher or someone says the wrong thing to her?"

"Then I would say that this person is probably very sensitive."

"Sensitive?"

"Yes. That means she feels things more deeply than other people."

So that's what she was. Sensitive. Millie thought about that for a while. "Mama, would you say that a person who is sensitive is special?"

"I would say that a person who is sensitive is very special." Her mother leaned over and kissed Millie's forehead.

Sensitive. Millie repeated the word over in her mind. She would write it down in her notebook first thing in the morning.

5

The Big Fight

The next day turned out to be one of the worst days of Millie's life. Miss Brennan chose her to be classroom monitor.

A monitor was not a good thing to be in Miss Brennan's class. While Miss Brennan was out of the room, you had to write the names of the talkers on the blackboard. If you wrote the names down, you were a tattletale. If you didn't and the room was noisy, Miss Brennan yelled at you for not being a good monitor, and everyone had to write *I will not talk* five hundred times.

Millie walked up to the front of the room, hoping that the class would behave. But the second Miss Brennan was out the door, the usual bunch of troublemakers started yelling and running around the room. One by one Millie wrote their names on the blackboard. And one by one, as the kids sat down and behaved, Millie erased their names. She believed in giving second chances. O.C. Goodwin and Howard Hall were walking on top of the desks and throwing erasers. Millie wrote the names *O.C. Goodwin* and *Howard Hall* on the board.

Howard Hall sat down, and Millie erased his name. O.C. called out, "Hey, what do you think you're doing? Take my name off that board."

"Sit down and I will," said Millie.

"I'll sit down when I feel like it. Now take my name off."

The whole class was quiet now. Everyone was listening to the argument that was taking place.

O.C. curled his upper lip and made a fist.

"I said take my name off the board, or I'll knock your block off."

"Yea! Fight, fight," some of the kids yelled out.

Millie did not want to have her block knocked off, but she didn't want the kids to think she could be threatened either.

"All you have to do is sit down," said Millie, "and I'll erase your name." She was giving him an out. Why didn't he take it?

"Erase it now, or I'll get you after school," O.C. said. He was shaking his fist at her. Not only was O.C. a troublemaker, he was also a bully. Some of the kids in the class kept him supplied

with notebook paper all year so he wouldn't bother them. If O.C. said he was going to get her, Millie was sure he was going to get her.

Millie was thinking that she'd leave O.C.'s name on the board until the last minute. Just to let him know that he couldn't scare her. When she heard Miss Brennan approaching, she would erase his name.

But O.C. wouldn't stop talking. He wouldn't stop telling Millie to erase his name . . . or else. Millie didn't see or hear Miss Brennan walking into the room. It was too late for any erasing now.

Miss Brennan looked at the blackboard. "O.C. Goodwin," she read out loud. Then she turned to O.C. and said, "Young man, you will write *I will not talk* five hundred times. And it's due tomorrow."

O.C. curled his lip again and held up his fist at Millie. In a voice loud enough for Millie to hear, but not loud enough for Miss Brennan to hear, he said, "I'll beat you to a pulp."

Once again Millie was the first one in line and the first one out of the building. Once again she was running home from school. She ran all the way, without stopping even once to see if O.C. was following her. She didn't stop until she was safely in her apartment, the door closed behind her.

6

Will O.C. Say OK?

It was eight o'clock Sunday night, and Millie was getting dressed for school. She had just finished eating breakfast—a bowl of Wheaties with sliced bananas—and now she was in her room picking out the clothes she would wear to sleep and to school the next morning.

Millie had spent a good part of the day figuring out a plan that would make it possible for her to sleep late and still get to school early. It was important to leave early so she could walk with the kids from her apartment building. O.C. would never beat her up with all those witnesses.

The plan Millie decided upon worked like this: She would do away with eating breakfast and getting dressed in the morning. She could take care of all that the night before. The time she saved in the morning could be better used for sleeping.

Millie put on clean underwear and bobby socks, and a freshly ironed dress from her closet. She

36

unbraided her hair and after brushing it out, she combed it straight down and pinned each side back with a barrette. By doing this, she saved even more time because now her mother wouldn't have to bother braiding her hair in the morning.

Millie stood in front of the mirror and was very pleased with what she saw. She saw a girl who was dressed and ready for school. And here it was, only Sunday night. She would have to tell Sandy about her plan. Sandy would appreciate it because she always had trouble waking up for school.

Millie climbed into bed very carefully so she wouldn't wrinkle her dress. Before she went to sleep, she reminded herself not to toss and turn, and to sleep straight instead of all curled up. Sleep straight, she kept telling herself. Sleep straight.

The next thing she knew, there was a knock on the door, and her father was calling, "It's eight o'clock, Millie. Time to get up."

"OK," Millie said as she curled up and went back to sleep. And because of those extra stolen minutes, it was a delicious sleep she fell into.

Another knock on the door came all too soon. It was her father again. "Millie, are you getting dressed?"

Millie jumped out of bed. "I'm dressed," she called back to him. She put on her shoes and went to the bathroom. She had forgotten to allow time for that in her plan.

Millie's father had already left for the furniture factory, and her mother was in the kitchen. Millie went in to say good morning and good-bye. She was ready for school—and for O.C. Goodwin.

"Good morning," said Millie.

"Good morning," said Mrs. Cooper. She was sitting at the table, drinking a glass of Ovaltine and working on a crossword puzzle from yesterday's newspaper.

"Good-bye," said Millie. "I'm going now."

"What about breakfast?" Mrs. Cooper asked without looking at her.

"I ate breakfast last night," said Millie.

Mrs. Cooper looked up from the newspaper. When she saw Millie, she could only stare. "My God," she said finally, "you look like you slept with your clothes on."

"I did," Millie said proudly. "I got dressed last night after I ate breakfast. And I was able to sleep late, and now I don't have anything to do— except leave for school."

Millie waited for her mother to tell her what a clever idea that was. But instead she said, "Go back and change. You can't go to school looking like that."

"Looking like what?" Millie asked. She looked

at herself in the dining-room mirror. True, her dress had a few wrinkles that it didn't have last night. But it looked OK.

"And comb your hair while you're at it," Mrs. Cooper ordered.

"But I'll be late." Millie thought about O.C. Goodwin.

"If you hurry, you can still make it."

Millie looked in her closet, but couldn't find anything to wear that she liked. So she just picked out a dress she could put on quickly. It had puffed sleeves. If there was one thing Millie hated, it was a dress with puffed sleeves.

She put it on anyway, adjusted the barrettes in her hair, grabbed her jacket, and ran out of the building. By this time there were no crowds of kids to walk with, so Millie had to run. She ran alone, wondering if O.C. was lurking in an alley or a hallway, ready to make his move.

Sandy was waiting for Millie at the corner of Thirteenth and Millard.

"You're late, Millie Cooper," Sandy called to her.

"I woke up late," Millie told her. She decided not to say anything about her plan. "Have you seen O.C. anywhere?"

"Oh, he probably forgot all about you by now," Sandy said.

"I'm not taking any chances," said Millie,

sticking close to Sandy and looking around for signs of O.C.

Millie and Sandy made it to Room 210 just before the nine o'clock tardy bell rang. O.C. was already in his seat, and when Millie looked at him, he sneered at her. He had not forgotten.

During arithmetic, while the rest of the class concentrated on the table of sevens, Millie made an important decision. She would not run from O.C. any longer. Two days of running from him was enough. She was not going to do it for the rest of her life. If he wanted to beat her up, then he would have to do it now and get it over with. Unless, of course, she could change his mind. Unless she could get him to think about something else.

When it came time to line up for lunch, Millie didn't rush to be first. She took her time walking down the stairs and waited for O.C. at the door.

"Hey, O.C.," she said.

"What do you want?" He glared at her.

"Do you have any comic books at home?"

"Yeah. Why?"

"Well, I have some too. Some real good ones. Do you want to trade?"

"Maybe."

"Look. Why don't I bring my comic books to school after lunch, and you bring yours, and we'll trade. OK?" Millie held her breath and waited for O.C.'s answer.

41

"Yeah, OK," said O.C.

"Really?" asked Millie.

"I said OK, didn't I?" said O.C.

"Sure, O.C. I'll see you after lunch."

That afternoon Millie walked home with Sandy. She didn't have to run. A boy who was going to trade comic books with her certainly wouldn't beat her to a pulp.

Millie picked out a Superman, a Wonder Woman, a Batman and two Captain Marvels. They were not her best comic books, but they weren't her worst ones either. And they all still had their covers.

Her father had brought them home from the barbershop the last time he went for a haircut. That's how Millie got her comic books—from the barber, who always gave her father his old ones when he got his new ones, and from trading. She rarely bought any. At ten cents a copy, her mother thought they were a waste of money.

Millie tucked the comic books under her arm when she was ready to leave after lunch.

"Are you taking those to school?" asked Mrs. Cooper. She didn't believe that school was a place for such junk.

"I'm going to trade with O.C. Goodwin," said Millie. And she told her mother how O.C. wanted to beat her up for writing his name on the blackboard, and how she talked him into trading comic books instead.

"Do you know what you did?" asked Mrs. Cooper. "You used psychology on O.C. Goodwin."

"I did?" said Millie. "No kidding?"

"He doesn't want to beat you up anymore, does he?"

"Hey, you're right," said Millie. "I did use psychology."

Millie knew how to use psychology—another thing that made her special. She wrote the word down on a piece of paper so she'd be sure to remember it. She even surprised her mother by spelling it correctly.

7

Rocket in Your Pocket

It was a lousy trade. For Millie's five quality comic books, O.C. gave her five copies of The Human Torch—none with covers. Ordinarily Millie would never have made such a bad trade. A comic book with a cover was worth at least two without covers. And Millie didn't even like The Human Torch. He was always on fire, and he wasn't really human. But under the circumstances, Millie felt that a happy O.C. was more important than a fair trade.

And O.C. *was* happy. Millie thought he even smiled at her once. He spent most of the afternoon reading the comic books, which he had hidden inside his geography book. Millie figured that Miss Brennan knew about the comic books, but O.C. didn't cause her any trouble that afternoon, so she pretended not to notice.

Millie and Sandy took a nice leisurely walk

home from school. Because of O.C. Goodwin, they hadn't done that in a long time.

"Did you start your 'Special' composition yet?" Millie asked.

"Not yet," said Sandy. "But I know what I'm going to write. I'll tell how dependable and responsible I am, how I get dinner started before my mother and father get home from work, and how I help around the house. It was my mother's idea. What about you? Do you know how you're special yet?"

"I'm still finding out," said Millie.

They walked into the candy store, and after a lot of decision making, Millie and Sandy each bought a pair of red wax lips. On the way out Millie put two pennies in the pistachio-nut machine. She got a whole handful of red nuts and shared half of them with Sandy.

They walked along, sucking on the salted nuts before splitting the shells open with their fingernails. They split their nails in the process, and red dye got all over their fingers. Now that Millie no longer had O.C. to worry about, it was just like old times.

Millie walked in through the back door. Today the kitchen smelled of cloves and nutmeg because her mother was baking a carrot cake. Mrs.

Cooper's carrot cakes were her specialty. Almost everyone asked for the recipe when they tasted her cake, and she willingly gave it out. Millie liked her mother's chocolate cake better, but the carrot cake wasn't so bad once you got used to it.

"Can I help?" Millie asked, dropping her books on the table and taking off her coat.

"You can grate a few more of these carrots for me," said Mrs. Cooper. "I want to try something a little different today as an experiment—more raisins and less sugar."

Millie washed her hands and picked up two carrots—one for eating and one for grating. Millie liked carrots. They were supposed to be good for your eyes. Maybe if she ate enough of them, she'd be able to see in the dark. She took a bite of one carrot and began grating the other. She liked to rub the carrot on one side of the grater and watch it come out in small pieces on the other side.

"This is fun," said Millie.

"You can grate for me anytime," said Mrs. Cooper. "Just be careful."

Millie took another bite and continued grating. She was chewing and grating, grating and chewing. And then— "Ouch!" cried Millie. "I think I just grated my knuckles." She looked at her knuckles and saw that she had scraped a little skin off one of them. It was bleeding slightly. She showed it to her mother.

"Just wash it off," said Mrs. Cooper. "It'll be OK. And I'll finish up."

"What if some of my skin and blood got into the carrots?" said Millie, loving the sound of the words *skin and blood.*

"The cake will taste better that way," said Mrs. Cooper.

"Ick," said Millie, enjoying herself even more.

Millie washed and dried her wounded knuckle and took the wax lips from her pocket. She put them on and sat down on the window seat. She sat there, wearing the lips and hugging herself. Things were picking up and she was feeling good. O.C. wasn't angry with her anymore, and so far she knew two ways in which she was special.

"How are you coming along on your composition?" It was as if her mother could read her thoughts.

Millie took the lips off. "I'm getting some ideas," she said. "But I really need that Rocket to write them with."

Millie waited hopefully for the right response from her mother. But none came, so she put the lips back on and stared out the window.

Mr. Cooper came home on time that evening. Millie was glad that he didn't get tied up in traffic. As soon as he walked into the kitchen, she could see how relaxed and happy he was. He handed her the newspaper and began picking the nuts off the top of the carrot cake while Millie checked the weather forecast.

"Darn it, still no snow," she said.

"Some things are more important than snow," said Mr. Cooper. He took a paper bag out of his coat pocket and gave it to Millie. One look at her father's face, one feel of the paper bag, and Millie knew what it was. She just knew. She looked inside the bag, and sure enough. There was the Rocket! A Chute Silver Reynolds Rocket!

"Oh, Daddy," cried Millie, jumping up and down. "Thank you, thank you, thank you." She flung her arms around his neck and then ran over to show the pen to her mother.

"Look, Mama, isn't it beautiful? I can't believe I actually have it. And it's just in time for my composition." She jumped up and down some more.

Mrs. Cooper examined the pen and smiled. "I had a hunch you'd weaken," she said to Mr. Cooper. "But it's very pretty. I just hope it works."

"Sure it works," Millie said, and she wrote her name on the bag. She wrote her name all over the bag. The pen didn't skip, it didn't leak, and it didn't goop. She let her mother try it, her father, too. Mr. Cooper drew lovely flowers along the border of the front page of the *Chicago Daily News*.

Millie spent the rest of the evening singing the Rocket song and admiring her new pen.

She sang the song with Sandy on the way to school the next morning. Millie couldn't wait for a chance to use her new pen.

The first subject was arithmetic, so Millie had to write her tables with a pencil. Miss Brennan never allowed anything but pencil for arithmetic. After arithmetic came spelling. Yesterday they had used the dictionary to find the definitions for the week's spelling words. Today they had to use each spelling word in a sentence. For once Millie looked forward to writing a heading. With her Rocket she wrote:

Millicent Cooper   November 19, 1946
Grade 3B   Room 210   Lawson School
Spelling Sentences

She loved the feel of the pen between her fingers, how easily it wrote. The ballpoint was truly a wonderful invention.

Millie was now ready to write her first sentence. She wrote the number one and put a period after it. The period was more like a glob of ink. Millie was shocked. She didn't know if it was a leak or a goop. She decided that whatever it was, it happened only because her pen was new and so full of ink. There were a few more globs of ink on her paper, but all in all, the pen wrote well and Millie was delighted.

While Millie was writing with her Rocket, she noticed Marlene Kaufman watching her. Marlene had begun writing with a fountain pen lately. Millie wondered why she wasn't using her Rocket anymore.

"I noticed that you've got a Reynolds Rocket," Marlene Kaufman said to Millie on the playground during recess. Millie was sitting on a swing. Sandy was swinging next to her, but Millie was sitting still. Swinging made her dizzy.

"My father bought it for me yesterday," she answered.

"I used to have one, too," said Marlene, "but I threw it away. They're no good."

"What?" Millie asked.

"Those Rockets. They're no good. They don't work."

"They do too," said Millie. "Mine works fine." She didn't mention the ink globs.

"It does now, but you'll see. It won't last long."

"It will too," said Millie. "It'll last for fifteen years."

"Fifteen years, my foot," said Marlene, and she walked away.

"I heard that," said Sandy. She scraped her

shoes on the gravel to stop the swing. "Just because her pen wasn't any good, it doesn't mean yours isn't."

"Sure," said Millie. "And besides, she probably didn't even know how to take care of it." Millie was not going to let Marlene Kaufman spoil the good feeling she had about her Rocket.

"Swing me?" Sandy asked.

Millie got up and gave Sandy a few gentle pushes. Once the swing got off to a good start, Millie began singing:

> *Got a Rocket in your pocket?*
> *If you do, don't sock it.*

As the swing went higher, Sandy joined in and they sang together:

> *Or you won't have a Rocket*
> *In your pocket*
> *Anymore.*

8

Trip to the Bottom of the Lake

The pen didn't leak or goop at all the next day. It skipped. Millie was trying to answer questions about Sir Francis Drake at the end of the chapter in her history book, but the ink just wouldn't come out right. Parts of letters were missing, parts of words were missing. One time *Sir Francis Drake* came out *Sir Francis rake.* Millie had to go back and try to fill in the missing parts, but that didn't always work.

Millie shook the pen and tried to get it to write on a piece of scratch paper. It still skipped.

Marlene Kaufman saw Millie's trouble and sent her a note. It probably says *I told you so,* Millie said to herself as she unfolded the paper. But the note didn't say *I told you so.* It said: *Warm it up. Roll it between your hands. Sometimes it stops working if it gets too cold.*

Millie rolled the Rocket between her hands. She

rolled it and blew on the point. She tried writing. It worked! The ink was flowing again. She flashed Marlene Kaufman a smile of gratitude. It seemed that Marlene really did know how to take care of a Rocket.

Millie finished the rest of the questions about Sir Francis Drake. And whenever the pen began to skip, she rolled it between her hands, and it worked again.

The next day, Thursday, Miss Brennan made an announcement. "From this day forward, ballpoint pens will not be allowed in this class. I will not accept any papers written with a ballpoint. They're impossible to read, and I will not go blind trying."

Millie couldn't be sure, but she thought Miss Brennan looked her way when she said "They're impossible to read."

But Miss Brennan didn't have to worry. Millie wouldn't be handing in any more papers written with a ballpoint pen. Her Rocket wasn't writing.

After a day of skipping, it absolutely refused to write. Millie did everything she could to get the ink flowing again. She kept it warm in her pocket, she rolled it between her hands, she shook it, she blew on the point, she even wrapped it in a towel and kept it on the radiator overnight. Nothing.

Millie couldn't figure it out. What was wrong with the pen anyway? It was supposed to work for fifteen years. Millie still had fourteen years and 363 days to go. It wasn't fair. And now her "Special" composition wouldn't be special.

Millie felt that she should have listened to her mother. The pen was a waste of money, an extravagant gimmick. And her father— He wasted three dollars and ninety-eight cents, plus tax, just to make her happy. For all that money she should have gotten more than two days of happiness.

Millie couldn't bear to look at her Rocket. She kept it in her desk all during school. On the way home from school after Sandy turned off down her street, Millie tried to figure out what to do with the pen. She couldn't keep it any longer. She had to get rid of it.

Millie considered the idea of losing her pen. She pulled the Rocket halfway out of her pocket so it would accidentally fall out while she was walking. The pen fell back into her pocket instead. When she reached the alley near her building, she thought about dropping the pen in a garbage can. But the garbage . . . ? No, the Rocket deserved something better.

Millie was relieved when her mother and father didn't ask about the pen that night, and neither of them asked to borrow it. She was also relieved when bedtime came around—so she could sleep away her unhappiness.

Millie got into her pajamas and picked out the clothes she would wear the next day. She placed them on top of the radiator so everything would be nice and warm in the morning. She went into the bathroom to wash up, and that's when the idea came to her. She knew just what she would do with her Rocket. She went back to the bedroom to get her pen, and a few minutes later she was standing in front of the sink, looking down the drain.

Millie held the pen over the drain. She let it fall through the dark opening in the sink—down, down, to the very bottom of the earth. Or at least to the bottom of Lake Michigan.

"Good-bye, dear Rocket," she called after it.

9

Second Chance

It was too late. From the moment the pen left her fingers, Millie was sorry about what she had done. She didn't want the pen at the bottom of the lake. She loved her Rocket and wanted to keep it— even if it didn't work. And maybe it would have worked again, someday, if she had given it another chance. But the pen was gone now, and she'd never know. How she wished she could have it back.

Millie stared at the drain. Why did she always do everything in a rush—without thinking things through? First she rushed into getting the pen, even though it wasn't perfected. And then she rushed into getting rid of it, rushed into dropping it down the drain. Her mother hated to throw money down the drain, and that's exactly what Millie did.

Without her Rocket Millie felt empty-handed

when she went to school on Friday. In the afternoon Miss Brennan stood in front of the room with an armful of construction paper and patterns for turkeys, Indians, and Pilgrim hats. "I think, class, that this might be a good time to begin our Thanksgiving decorations."

The kids all cheered at the announcement, not only because Thanksgiving decorations were fun to make, but also because you got out of doing all the regular work. Millie was glad about the patterns. With patterns she could draw as well as anyone.

Millie was not good in art. The only things she could draw well were houses and trees. Along the top of the blackboard in back of the room, among the rest of the October paintings, hung Millie's painting of a house and tree. It was very much like her September picture of a house and tree, except in September she painted green grass and green leaves on the tree; and in October she made the leaves gold and brown, and the tree was on the other side of the house.

Miss Brennan seemed to have forgotten about the November paintings, and Millie thought it was a good thing. She just couldn't draw any more houses and trees.

"I'm going to pass out the paper and patterns now," Miss Brennan said. "But we don't have enough patterns to go around, so you'll have to share. And you'll find paste and scissors on the back table."

"Do we have to use patterns, or can we draw our own pictures?" Marlene Kaufman asked. Marlene Kaufman was good in art.

"You may draw your own," said Miss Brennan.

It took a long time for the patterns to be passed around, and while Millie was waiting to get one, she took a black crayon and made an outline of her hand on a piece of construction paper. Her hand was going to be a turkey. Her fingers were the feathers, and her thumb was the turkey's head and neck. She added the legs.

Sandy used her hand as a pattern, too. Only her hand became an Indian head. The fingers were his headdress, and the hand was his face. Millie and Sandy compared their pictures, and by that time they each had a pattern to use.

Millie was outlining a Pilgrim hat and Sandy was outlining a turkey when Howard Hall called out, "Hey, Miss Brennan, O.C.'s got a turkey and a hat, and he's not sharing."

O.C. gave Howard Hall a dirty look and threw him a turkey.

While everyone was busy drawing, cutting, and pasting, Miss Brennan went to the back board to remove the October paintings. Then she walked up to the front of the room to make another announcement.

"December paintings will be due next Wednesday, the day before Thanksgiving. That way we'll have nice, new paintings waiting for us when we come back, and when we take down our Thanksgiving decorations, the room won't look so naked."

Everyone laughed at the thought of a naked room. Everyone except Millie. Now she had another problem to worry about—what to draw for her December painting.

"You can draw a house and a tree in the snow, and a snowman in front," Sandy suggested on the way home.

"That's so babyish," said Millie. "I can't keep drawing baby pictures. I want to draw something of beauty and value." Millie had heard her mother use that expression one time when they were at the Art Institute, and she liked it.

They stopped at the candy store, and they each bought some wax teeth. After she dropped Sandy off at her corner, Millie wore her wax teeth home. She came up the back way, and even before she walked into the kitchen, she could smell the supper cooking: chicken and soup and lots of other good things. Friday night suppers were the best of all.

Millie opened the door and went inside. There

in front of her stood Mrs. Cooper holding— No, it couldn't be! But it was. Millie was taken by such surprise that her wax teeth almost fell out of her mouth. How could her mother have gotten it from the bottom of the lake? It was a miracle! Her wish had come true.

"Can you tell me how your pen got into the pipe?" asked Mrs. Cooper. "It stopped up the sink."

Millie took her teeth out. "Uh . . . I guess it fell in when I was trying to see if it wrote underwater."

"See if you can take better care of it from now on," said Mrs. Cooper, and she gave Millie's Rocket back to her.

"Oh, I will," said Millie, holding the pen close to her. "I'll never let it out of my sight."

Millie skipped happily into the bathroom to see if she could figure out how her mother found her Rocket. She looked in the drain and then under the sink. No wonder. The pipe curved. It didn't go straight down. Why hadn't she noticed before?

Millie went into her bedroom and tried writing with the pen, hoping that the overnight stay in the pipe had done something to get it working again. Nothing had changed. The pen still didn't write. But at least she had her Rocket back, and that's what mattered.

Millie spent part of Sunday trying to fix the Rocket by running hot water over the point, and most of the day trying to draw something for her December painting. She tried drawing the polar bears she had seen at Brookfield Zoo, ice skaters skating on a frozen pond in Garfield Park, and kids sledding down the hill on Douglas Boulevard. But everything looked one way in her imagination and quite another way on her paper.

By Monday her pen still didn't write. Her art paper was full of holes from all the erasing she did, and she had to get another sheet. She would have to try again. Maybe she could come up with something by Wednesday.

Instead of doing work in the afternoon, the class sang Thanksgiving songs. Millie sat on her pen, trying to warm it up, while Miss Brennan sat at the piano and began playing "Over the River and Through the Woods." It's a song about going to visit Grandmother's house on a horse-drawn sleigh. When they got to the part about the white and drifting snow, Millie looked out the window. There wasn't even a single snowflake in sight.

They sang a song about gathering together to ask the Lord's blessing, and then Miss Brennan got up in front of the room to teach the class a new song. It was all about pumpkin pie and turkeys who did a lot of gobbling. She stood there,

singing with a quivering and vibrating voice, trying to sound like an opera singer. O.C. Goodwin and Howard Hall were snickering in the last row. Sandy and Millie were trying to stifle their giggles. For some reason Millie didn't think that opera singers sang about turkeys.

Millie got to work on her art paper right after supper. She sat down at the dining-room table, drawing and erasing and listening to the radio. She worked right through "The Lone Ranger," "Inner Sanctum," and "The Voice of Firestone." But for all her efforts, there was nothing in front of her except a worn-out sheet of art paper.

"I think you'd better get to sleep," said Mrs. Cooper. "You can try again tomorrow."

But Millie could barely hear her mother. She was already beginning to fall asleep in the middle of the "Lux Radio Theater."

10

So Many Shades of Blue

Millie was always grateful that she had inherited her father's blue eyes. Now she was beginning to wish that she had inherited his artistic talent instead.

She went through three sheets of art paper trying to draw something of beauty and value. By Tuesday night she gave up.

"Daddy," Millie asked, "can you draw something for me? I tried and tried, and nothing comes out right."

"You won't get any satisfaction out of something *I* draw," said her father.

"I don't care about satisfaction," said Millie. "I just don't want to get yelled at."

"Do you think it's right for you to get credit for something I do?" he asked.

"But I'll do all the painting myself. I just need help with the drawing. Please, Daddy. Otherwise I'll get a U in art."

Mr. Cooper thought for a moment, then he looked at his watch, and he looked at Millie.

"OK," he said, getting up from his chair near the radio. "Just this once."

"It's got to be a winter scene," said Millie. "And don't make it too good."

Mr. Cooper sat down next to Millie at the table and, with Millie's pencil, began sketching. Millie admired the short, quick strokes her father made. Almost effortlessly—with the very pencil that was nothing but lead in Millie's hand, on the very same paper that Millie had used—he created a small boy skating on a frozen pond.

Mr. Cooper finished the picture in no time at all, and then it was Millie's turn to do the painting. With her temperas, she began painting the boy. She gave him yellow hair because, except for Ronald Van Buskirk, who sat behind her, all the boys in her class had ordinary dark hair. Millie wanted her boy to have yellow hair like Ronald Van Buskirk's.

The boy in her picture would wear red earmuffs to match his red jacket, Millie decided, and would skate under a powder blue sky. She saved the sky for last. To get powder blue, Millie mixed dark blue and white in the cap of one of the jars of paint. She mixed just the right amount of each color to get the shade she wanted. It was a lovely shade of blue, and she began painting.

When Millie ran out of powder blue, she mixed up some more and began painting again. The blue was too dark, so she added white. Now the blue was too light, and she had to make it darker. Millie kept mixing and painting, but she could never come up with the same shade twice. She held the painting in front of her. The blues were different, but Millie thought the sky looked kind of nice that way. She would paint the rest of the sky with different shades of blue and not worry about matching. The only thing she'd have to worry about was Miss Brennan. Miss Brennan liked everything neat. She'd probably say the sky was messy with all those blues. Maybe she would even refuse to hang the painting with the others.

In the morning Millie took her Rocket from under her pillow, where she'd kept it all night, and put it in the pocket of her jacket. She checked to make sure that her painting was dry, then she signed her name in pencil in the lower left-hand corner. She dated it *November 27, 1946.* For art work she didn't need a heading. She rolled her picture up and took it to school, determined that this time, even if Miss Brennan said something mean about her sky, Millie wouldn't cry. Instead, she would imagine the boy lifting up Miss Brennan's wig with a window pole, and she would laugh inside her mind.

Room 210 did the usual afternoon's work while

Miss Brennan hung the December paintings along the top of the back board. She hung Millie's right in the middle of the others.

At fifteen minutes before three o'clock, Miss Brennan asked everyone to turn around and look at the paintings. She walked along, commenting, as she always did, on each painting. She liked Marlene Kaufman's use of color. Sandy Feinman made her figures too small. When Miss Brennan approached Millie's painting, Millie held her breath. It seemed to her that Miss Brennan stared at the painting for a long time.

"Millicent Cooper," Miss Brennan read the name on the painting. Millie didn't like her tone of voice. She called upon her imaginary boy and his window pole. The boy had Ronald Van Buskirk's hair.

Miss Brennan turned towards Millie and said, "Do you know what I like about this painting, Millicent?"

"Huh?" said Millie. Was she hearing right?

"I like the sky," said Miss Brennan.

In a puff the boy and his window pole disappeared.

"The sky looks so real," Miss Brennan continued. And then she directed her attention to the rest of the class. "You know, class, the sky, the real sky, is not just one shade of blue. It is many, many shades of blue all blended together."

Millie could not believe it. The part of the painting that Miss Brennan liked best was not the part her father did—not the boy or the frozen pond. What she liked was the sky. *Her* sky.

"You're very artistic, Millicent," said Miss Brennan.

"Huh?" Millie said softly. Artistic? Me? Millie Cooper?

It was a wonderful word. Millie tried it out while she gathered her books together. She tried it out while she waited in line for the three o'clock bell to ring. She loved the feel of the word in her mouth, the way her tongue and teeth worked together to get that sound. *Artistic.*

The bell rang and as the class filed out the door, Miss Brennan called to them. "Don't forget your 'Special' compositions, class. Due after Thanksgiving."

Oh, she wouldn't forget. Not Millie. How could she? She had so many things to write about. She felt the Rocket lying warm and cozy in the pocket of her jacket. A Rocket in her pocket. Maybe the pen would write again someday, and maybe it never would. But it didn't matter. She was special without the pen. She was sensitive, she knew how to use psychology, and now she was artistic. And come to think of it, she had become a pretty fast runner from all her running experience this month, and she was a natural born speller. Why, she was special in lots of ways. She didn't need a pen to tell her that.

The school doors opened, and everyone burst out into the street filled with that wonderful sense of freedom that comes when you get a four-day vacation.

O.C. Goodwin called out to her, "See you next week, Millie."

The air felt brisk and the day was cold and cloudy—just the way Millie liked a November day to be. She and Sandy skipped down the sidewalk, singing "Over the River and Through the Woods." They sang about the horse and the sleigh and the white and drifting snow.

Snow? Was it? Yes, it was! "It's snowing," Millie cried out. She and Sandy hugged each other and jumped up and down. Then they twirled around trying to catch the snowflakes that were now coming down thick and heavy.

"Did you know," said Sandy, "that no two snowflakes are exactly alike? You could have a million snowflakes and they'd all be different?"

"You could have a billion snowflakes and they'd all be different," Millie said. And she twirled around, with her face up towards the sky, catching the snowflakes in her mouth and on her nose and her eyelashes.

"You could have a trillion snowflakes," said Sandy, twirling along with Millie before she ran off down Millard Street.

"A zillion," Millie called out after her.

Sandy turned around and Millie waved. "Good-bye, Sandy Feinman."

Sandy smiled and waved back. "Good-bye, Millie Cooper. And happy Thanksgiving."

Other Novels by Charlotte Herman

WHAT HAPPENED TO HEATHER HOPKOWITZ?
OUR SNOWMAN HAD OLIVE EYES
THE DIFFERENCE OF ARI STEIN
THE THREE OF US
(in paperback, JUST WE THREE)